Being a Cat

A Tail of Curiosity

Words by MARIA GIANFERRARI
Pictures by PETE OSWALD

HARPER
An Imprint of HarperCollinsPublishers

ISBN 978-0-06-306792-9
The artist used cutout paper and scanned watercolor textures
to create the digital illustrations for this book.
22 23 24 25 26   RTLO   10 9 8 7 6 5 4 3 2 1
❖
First Edition

For Nancy and her cute clutter of kitties:
Jerry, Lulu & Keiko
—M.G.

To George and Crickette

—P.O.

Can you be like a cat?
Being a cat
is seeking—

watching,

wondering,

wandering,

surveying
everything
around you.

Can you search like a cat?

Perch high.

Look low.

Lurk under

and around.

What have you found?

Are you happy?

Trilllllll.

(In between,
preen.)

What's that over there . . . ?

Explore a drawer.

Discover clothes
and doze.

Stop
and smell the flowers—

nip,

flip,

tip!

(Preen
in between.)

Put to the test,
a box is simply the best.

Can you notice like a cat?

Observe—
angle and dangle.

Spot—
dive and dash.

Spy—
paw and claw.

Hide.

Surprise!

Tuckered and tired,
catnap in curious places—

(Preen
in between).

Here,

there,

anywhere,

everywhere!

Then scout like a cat—

investigate.

Inspect.

Inquire.

(In between, preen.)

How do you say I love you like a cat?

Jump.

Rub.

Bunt.

Twine.

Twist.

Wind.

Blink once,

then twice.

Knead.

Cuddle.

Curl,
like a question mark.

Are you really happy?
Purring is purr-fect.

DING . . . DONG

What's that?

Be curious,
like a cat.

Stick out your tongue!

Our tongues are soft and help us talk, taste, and swallow. **Cat tongues feel like rough sandpaper** because they're covered with backward-facing barbs made of keratin—the same stuff your hair and nails are made of. These claw-shaped spines work like combs, cleaning the cat's fur and distributing natural oils. Cat tongues curve like spoons for lapping liquid. Bye-bye, brush! Hello, spoon!

Sniff, sniff. What's your favorite smell?

Humans have millions of scent receptors, but **cats have smelling superpowers**: over 200 million scent receptors and multiple scent glands all over their bodies! They also have a Jacobson's organ in the roof of their mouths to help them analyze scents. When cats scratch something, they're "sign-posting," spreading their scent and marking territory. When cats rub their heads against you, it's called "bunting," which means they love you and they "own" you.

CAT'S MEOW!

Close your eyes. Pretend you have long whiskers on the sides of your face.

When you walk, your whiskers rub against things. **A cat's whiskers are full of sensitive nerve endings** that help them "see" the world around them. They detect changes in air currents like a radar detector, which helps them navigate their nighttime surroundings.

Scritch-scratch-snatch!

Are your fingernails sharp? They're good for scratching itches. **Cat claws are like tools:** sharp and curved at the ends for catching and killing prey, climbing, and defending themselves. When a cat walks, its claws are retracted, or pulled in, which helps it stalk and sneak up on prey.

TAILS

Can you express your emotions using your body and no words?

CATS TELL TALES WITH THEIR TAILS!

What does your mouth look like when you're happy?
A happy cat's tail sticks up straight like a pole.

How do you ask your friends to play without words?
A cat's tail curls like a question mark when it's feeling playful.

If you're angry, what do your eyes look like?

An irritated cat swishes its tails back and forth, like a windshield wiper. When it's angry, the cat's tail is stiff, straight up, and fluffed out.

What does your body look like when you're scared?

Cats tuck their tails between their back legs if they're scared.

LEAP LIKE A CAT!

CAThletes: Domestic and other wild cats have longer hind limbs, which help them spring into action to chase prey. Your cat might be able to jump more than five feet high and leap just as far!

CROUCH ON ALL FOURS.

BEND YOUR LEGS.

STRAIGHTEN YOUR ARMS.

SPRING!!

COOL CATS!

🐾 Feline means belonging to the cat family.

🐾 Baby cats are kittens.

🐾 A group of cats is a clowder or a clutter.

🐾 A tomcat is a domestic male cat; molly is its female equivalent.

🐾 A pregnant cat, or one that has kittens, is called a queen.